Monsters
and Mythical Creatures

Giants

Adam Woog

ReferencePoint
Press®

San Diego, CA

My thanks to the many friends whose suggestions
made this book better—especially Arlen Pringle.

© 2012 ReferencePoint Press, Inc.
Printed in the United States

For more information, contact:
ReferencePoint Press, Inc.
PO Box 27779
San Diego, CA 92198
www.ReferencePointPress.com

LIBRARY OF CONGRESS CATALOGING-IN-PUBLICATION DATA

Woog, Adam, 1953-
  Giants / by Adam Woog.
    p. cm. -- (Monsters and mythical creatures)
  Includes bibliographical references and index.
    ISBN-13: 978-1-60152-224-5 (hardback)
    ISBN-10: 1-60152-224-X (hardback)
  1. Giants--Juvenile literature. 2. Giants--Folklore. I. Title.
  GR560.W66 2012
  599.9'49--dc23
                                                                                2011026637

Contents

Giants Roam the Earth

Everyone knows what giants are: enormous and immensely powerful creatures. They often take human form. However, they are always far larger and stronger than any normal person.

Legends, myths, and other stories about giants can be found in virtually every culture around the world and throughout history. These stories have thrilled and captivated humankind for thousands of years and still do. This fascination is a universal feeling. Writer Carol Rose comments, "Few people could fail to have been fascinated by the story of some gigantic or monstrous being at some point in their lives."[1]

How Giants Were Born

A number of reasons account for the emergence and staying power of ancient stories about legendary and mythical giants. Perhaps the most common and widespread reason was, and still is, a deep and very natural human impulse. This impulse is the desire to explain how the world was created, how people and everything else in the world came to be, and what might lie beyond the tangible—that is, beyond what can be seen or heard or touched.

One way for ancient societies to explain the creation of the world was to imagine that supernatural creatures—including giants—were responsi-

> ## Did You Know?
>
> All around the world, giants are often portrayed as being very stupid or greedy.

ble. What else, they asked, could explain the existence of people, animals, mountains, trees, rivers, the heavens, rain, thunder, and drought?

Closely related to these creation stories is another cornerstone of legends about giants. This is their association with religious beliefs. A familiar example is the story of David and Goliath, as told in the Judeo-Christian Bible. This and other religious stories about giants are typically interpreted as demonstrating the eternal struggle between good and evil.

Still another reason for the development of legends about giants does not necessarily involve religion or creation. This is the desire to relate exciting stories about famous heroes of previous ages. Typically, these heroes are mighty warriors. The storytellers who related legends about these heroes, naturally enough, embellished and expanded their heroes' powers and adventures. As a result, the legends became more elaborate and detailed as they passed from generation to generation. For example, the legend of Finn McCool, the most famous of the many giants in Irish folklore, probably began as stories about a real-life warrior. In time the tales about this powerful but human hero grew to giant proportions.

Still another reason for the development of myths about giants was simply the urge to tell good stories—an urge that has always existed. Scary, funny, or strange tales about giants fascinated people in ancient times, and their popularity is still strong. In some cases these stories take the form of folk or fairy tales, such as "Jack and the Beanstalk," or tall tales about the larger-than-life exploits of Paul Bunyan, the strongest logger who ever lived. Further proof of the public's love of giants can be seen in more recent examples of popular culture. These range from books and movies to comics, advertisements, games, and more.

Common Threads

Ancient or new, the giants in stories appear in many shapes and forms. There is apparently no end to their variety. They can be

> ## Did You Know?
>
> Some legendary giants look like enormous humans, but some are said to have strange features such as a serpent's tail or many heads.

Tom Thumb encounters a sleeping giant in this illustration of the famous English folktale. Stories featuring giants can be found in virtually every culture.

stupid and greedy, like the giant in "Jack and the Beanstalk." But they can also be smart and sweet, like the giant in Roald Dahl's book *The BFG* (Big Friendly Giant). Some legendary giants are generous and helpful, such as the Jentil, who taught farming and metalworking to the Basque people in what is now Spain. Others are terrifying, cruel, and hideous, such as the Cyclopes of Greek legend. Some giants are divine, such as those that appear in countless myths around the world. In contrast, some giants are distinctly earthbound, like Paul Bunyan and his faithful companion, Babe the Blue Ox.

Did You Know?

The giants in many myths are heroes who kill evil creatures, but some giants *are* the evil ones.

On the other hand, despite the diversity of legends about giants around the world and throughout time, they have a surprising number of themes and ideas in common. For example, many myths depict giants as gods who form the world from their body parts. Examples of this theme include Pangu from China and Ymir from the Norse regions of northern Europe. Also, a number of ancient stories say that giants came into being as the children of intermarriage between gods and mortals. And still other giants appear in religious stories, such as the legend of a flood that once covered the world. Typically, the giants in such stories survive because they are so huge that their heads stay above water. These flood legends can be found in many cultures, from the Middle East to South America.

Did Giants Really Exist?

Many people who are interested in unusual or supernatural subjects believe that giants once really did roam the earth—and perhaps still do. These people claim to have evidence of their beliefs. However, there is no definitive proof that giants really existed—except, that is, for people with gigantism, a rare medical condition that causes humans to grow abnormally tall.

> # Did You Know?
>
> The words *giant* and *gigantic* come from the Gigantes, enormous brothers who were part of Greek mythology.

Over the years, the topic has been the focus of a great deal of misinformation, misunderstanding, or outright fraud. One example of how claims about giants can be misinterpreted or exaggerated concerns a report from the late nineteenth century about giant skeletons allegedly found in an old burial mound in Ohio. People interested in supernatural or unusual phenomena say that this report must be true, since it was mentioned in 1891 in a respected magazine, *Nature*.

However, skeptics counter this argument by noting that the article was apparently nothing more than a review of a book on gigantism. Despite this skeptical view, the story's accuracy has been taken for granted by a great many people. In recent years the Internet has helped spread the story (and belief in it) to proportions that are, well, giant.

Despite the uncertainty about the truth of the existence of giants, stories about them are still exciting and fascinating. Clearly, there is something about legendary giants that continues to have a firm grip on the public's imagination.

Chapter 1

Creation Myths and Religious Legends

Questions about creation have always been part of human culture and of the religious faiths that have emerged from various societies. People in every culture in the world, and in every period since the start of recorded history and possibly even before that time, have been curious about the origins of what they see and touch. They asked and still ask: Where did the world come from? What, or who, formed the sky, the earth, the lakes, rivers, and oceans? How did animals come to be? These queries naturally led (as they still do) to another question that society finds especially important: *Why* was everything created?

Today humankind is still trying to answer such questions and to extend its understanding of what lies beyond the immediate world. Religious people believe that a deity created the earth and continues to direct it. Others observe the origin of the universe and everything in it from a scientific viewpoint.

Few today would believe ancient myths about the human race springing from a magical tree, or mountains and lakes emerging from the body parts of a giant. But such stories were once commonplace. And these stories, as well as the religious beliefs that grew from them, nearly always included giants. To these ancient people, only giants, or giants that gods had created, would have the power to create the whole world and everything in it.

Greco-Roman Creation and Religious Myths

The Greek mythologies are good examples of how giants figure prominently in creation and religion myths. Even in a relatively small region like Greece, a great many overlapping stories emerged there in ancient times. (The Roman Empire later adapted many of the Greek myths, changing them slightly and giving the gods new names. For example, the Greek sea god Poseidon was renamed Neptune.)

According to the most widespread Greek legend, before people existed there was a shapeless, empty darkness called Chaos. The only thing in it was Nyx, the giant winged goddess of night, who created the earth and sky out of two halves of an egg. Nyx was apparently an enormous but benevolent giant. Statius, a Roman poet of the first century AD, described her as so large that she could envelop the sky in her cloak. He wrote, "Nox [Nyx] came on, and laid to rest the cares of men and the prowlings of wild beasts, and wrapped the heavens in her dusky [dark] shroud, coming to all with kindly influence."[2]

The extremely complex structure of Greece's religious mythology developed out of the story of Nyx and other similar creation stories. It included dozens of gods, goddesses, and semigods (half gods)—and many of them were giants. Together they controlled the world.

One group of gods was the Titans. Some stories pictured these 12 giants as monsters with 50 heads and 100 arms, but in other versions they looked like giant humans. They were very fierce and could throw boulders so hard that they created earthquakes, massive waves, and thunder.

Did You Know?

The Koran, the sacred book of Islam, states that Adam and Eve were once huge, but their descendants became smaller over time.

Cronus and Zeus

One of the Titans, Cronus, was especially powerful and brutal. He wanted to kill his father, the king of the skies, and take power. So Cronus cut off his father's genitals and threw them into the sea. The drops of blood formed the Greek islands, and from these islands came another group of giants, the Gigantes.

The Giants Who Stumble on Blackberry Bushes

Bulgaria, in eastern Europe, is a country with a long tradition of mythical giants. According to the ancient stories, dwarves lived on the earth long before modern humans. However, they were too small to defend themselves against wild animals. They died out, and God created giants called the Ispolini to take their place. These were the first two versions of humans to appear before the birth of modern people.

Many versions of the Ispolini story have survived. According to one, the giants had huge heads and stood about 10 feet (3m) tall. In other versions the Ispolini had three heads, a single eye in the middle of each forehead, and/or a single leg. The voices of the giants were so powerful that they could communicate with one another even between distant mountains. They lived in caves, fought often with dragons, and ate only raw meat. But the Ispolini had a weakness: a dread of blackberry bushes. The giants feared that they would trip over the berry bushes and be killed by their own tremendous weight.

Today huge mounds of stones dot the countryside in Bulgaria. Archaeologists think that these are the ruins of very old buildings, or perhaps burial sites. However, according to legend, the mounds are really the graveyards of the Ispolini.

Another of Cronus's terrible acts resulted from a prophecy that one of his sons would take his place. Cronus tried to prevent this by eating his children. But Cronus's wife hid one of his children, Zeus, by sending him to another land. When he grew up he returned to overthrow Cronus, but he needed the help of his siblings. Zeus secretly gave Cronus poison that made him vomit up his brothers and sisters, and together they conquered their father. Zeus later became the king of the gods and divided the universe among his siblings.

Another important giant in Greek mythology was Atlas. He was the king of Atlantis, an enormous mythological island that eventually sank into the sea. According to one version of the story, after losing a battle with Zeus, Atlas was condemned forever to hold up the heavens as punishment. In later centuries he became known for holding up the earth.

Norse Creation and Religious Myths

Far from sunny Greece, in the frigid far north of Europe, another society had its own set of creation and religious myths. This society was a group of tribes called the Norse. They lived in what is today Sweden, Norway, Finland, Denmark, Greenland, and Iceland.

The Norse creation story has many variations. According to one version, at first nothing in the world existed except for ice in the north and fire in the south. When a few pieces of ice fell in between these halves, they melted and created the water of life. The water, in turn, formed a giant called Ymir.

When Ymir died, the earth was made from his body. His blood formed the sea, his flesh was the earth, his skull was the sky, his bones were the mountains, and his hair formed the trees. Meanwhile, the sweat of the giant's armpit created two other gods, a man and a woman, who were the ancestors of more gods. In time these gods formed the first humans from tree trunks. Ymir's eyebrows became fences to enclose the land where these humans lived.

According to Greek mythology, the giant known as Atlas was forced to bear the weight of the heavens after losing a battle to Zeus, the king of the gods. As in this ancient sculpture, Atlas is often depicted holding Earth on his shoulders.

Norse religious mythology developed alongside this creation myth and expanded on it. If anything, the Norse system of gods was even more complex than the Greek legends. As with the Greeks, giant semigods figured prominently. These were the Jötunn, a name that probably comes from the ancient Norse word for "man-eater."

These enormous and tremendously strong creatures were the children of Ymir. They generally looked like humans, although some had claws, fangs, and monstrous faces, and some had many heads. Sometimes the Norse gods appeared in other forms as well. For example, Hrungnir, the strongest of all the giants, was made of stone. The *Prose Edda*, one of the great epics of Norse mythology, states, "Hrungnir had the heart which is notorious, of hard stone and spiked with three corners. . . . His head also was of stone; his shield too was stone, wide and thick."[3]

The semidivine Jötunn created and controlled the region's rugged weather and landscape. There were frost giants, fire giants, mountain giants, and more. The Norse believed that the Jötunn lived in Jötunnheim, one of the nine worlds that made up all creation. Jötunnheim had no trees, lakes, or other features and was divided into separate regions. For example, Muspelheim ("Fire Land") was a place of endless flames where the fire giant Surtr ruled. Another of these semigods was Thor, the god of lightning. Other deities, such as Odin, were considered full gods. The Jötunn battled the other gods and each other constantly. One of these battles was between Thor and a multiheaded giant named Thrivaldi ("Three Times Mighty"). When Thor killed Thrivaldi, the monster's nine heads were split apart and he died instantly.

> # Did You Know?
>
> According to a tale from ancient Ireland, giants and humans lived simultaneously in ancient times, sometimes peacefully and sometimes at war.

Ready to strike a fateful blow, Thor raises his hammer in this 1872 painting Thor's Fight with the Giants. *According to Norse mythology, the semigod Thor killed a giant nine-headed monster.*

Pangu: A Chinese Creation Myth

Many other creation myths involving giants have emerged from cultures around the world. For example, the ancient Middle Eastern realm of Babylonia had a legend about a giant goddess named Tiamat. In some versions of the legend, Tiamat warred with her children, who were also gigantic gods. One of them, the god of storms, killed her. He sliced her body in two, and the halves formed heaven and earth.

Many creation myths involving giants also come from China. China is a vast country, so it is no surprise that a number of cultures within its borders tell their own creation myths. The best known of these, one that was widespread across ancient China, concerns a giant god named Pangu.

In some ways the myth of Pangu closely resembles creation myths from other parts of the world. For example, it relates that before the world existed, there was nothing but chaos. Out of this chaos, a cosmic egg formed. Thousands of years later, the egg hatched Pangu.

Pangu was not immediately a giant. However, he grew remarkably fast. In some versions, he grew 6 feet (1.83m) a day for 18,000 years. Pangu then created the earth and sky by swinging a giant ax to divide the chaos, then stood between them to prevent their coming together again. Gradually, he pushed the two so far that they could never meet. This is similar to other legends such as the story of Atlas, who was forced to hold the sky up to keep heaven and hell apart.

When Pangu died, his breath formed the wind, his voice created thunder, his eyes became the sun and moon, and his body made the mountains. Pangu's blood turned into the rivers, his beard into the stars, his bones into valuable minerals, his sweat into the rain, and the fleas on his skin into all living creatures. Again, this is similar to many creation myths in which the body parts of giant gods became the features of world when they died.

An Australian Aboriginal Creation Story

Still other stories in which the body parts of giants formed the earth can be found in places like India and Australia. For example, one myth from India concerns Purusha, a 1,000-headed giant who was sacrificed by the gods and torn apart to create humans as well as the earth and its features, including trees, mountains, and rivers.

Meanwhile, in the northwestern part of Australia, the aboriginal (native) people have a creation myth about two giant brothers, both named Mungan. They were born in a region called Bagadjimbiri, and at first they looked like the wild dogs that Australians call dingoes.

The brothers grew until their heads touched the sky. They traveled all over, creating and naming all of the features of the landscape, as well as all of the animals and fish. They also finished creating people, who existed but were not yet complete.

The brothers changed into giants who looked like humans. But they got into an argument with a cat-man who was annoyed by their laughter. He killed them with a spear, but the brothers' mother, a goddess, drowned the cat-man. The brothers were reborn and turned into water snakes. Their spirits became clouds, which allowed rain to fall on the earth to make things grow.

> # Did You Know?
> The mythology of the ancient Aztecs included seven chief gods who were also giants.

Giants in Judeo-Christian Traditions

Many creation myths such as these incorporated giants into the more complex religious beliefs that developed along with them. One prominent example is the Judeo-Christian tradition.

There are many references to giants in the Old Testament of the Bible (the first part of the Christian holy book), which is also the holy book of the Jews. One of these references describes people called the Nephilim. As the book of Genesis (the first book of the Bible) describes them, "there were giants in the earth in those days; and also after that, when the sons of God came in unto the daughters of men, and they bare [bore] children to them, the same became mighty men which were of old, men of renown."[4]

The Nephilim are also mentioned several times later in the Bible. For example, in the book of Numbers, another of the books in the Old Testament, Jewish spies reported on their journeys. They said of the Nephilim, "And there we saw the giants, the sons of Anak . . . and we were in our own sight as grasshoppers, and so we were in their sight [as well]."[5]

However, the most familiar giant story in the Bible is that of David and Goliath. It is a classic example of good triumphing over evil. According to the book of Samuel, Goliath was the greatest warrior of a tribe called the Philistines. He is sometimes described as being 4 cubits and a span high, which would have made him roughly 6 feet 9 inches (2.06m) tall. However, other sources say he was 6 cubits and a span—making him over 9 feet (2.74m) tall.

In either case he and the other Philistine warriors gathered in preparation for a battle against another tribe, the Israelites. Rather than engage in full warfare, the Philistines sent Goliath out by himself, twice a day for 40 days, to challenge any Israelite who would fight him. A reward was offered to anyone who would fight Goliath, and a young man, David, took the challenge. The gigantic, club-wielding Goliath was terrifying, but David used his brain. From a distance, he shot a stone with a sling. It hit the giant in the forehead and killed him. David cut off Goliath's head in triumph, and the Philistines ran away. Later, David became king of the Israelites.

Many other giants appear in Jewish and Christian lore. Saint Christopher, later known as the patron saint of travelers, appears in some such stories from Christianity. In these stories Saint Christopher was sometimes depicted as a giant who carried travelers—including Jesus—across a dangerous river.

And the Jews of eastern Europe have a story about giant artificial men called Golems. According to legend, a Golem was made of clay and could do simple chores when certain words and phrases were invoked, but the creature was also dangerous if unchecked. When not under the control of a rabbi, a Golem could become violent, killing non-Jews and otherwise creating chaos.

Did You Know?

Part of a creation myth told by the Inuit people of Alaska and the far north of Canada tells how a giant girl who fell into the ocean died. Her fingers became the first sea animals.

Giants in Islamic Religious Traditions

Several references that appear in the Judeo-Christian Bible also appear in the Koran, the holy book of Islam. Notably, David is considered by Islam to be a major prophet. The Koran also mentions Adam and Eve, who in both the Koran and the Bible were the first humans. According to Islamic teachings, Adam and Eve were giants. *Sahih al-Bukhari*, a set of commentaries on the Koran dating from at least the ninth century, states, "The Prophet [Muhammad] said, 'Allah

David gives thanks to God after defeating Goliath and triumphantly cutting off the giant's head. This classic tale from the Bible is depicted here by the Italian artist Titian, circa 1488 to 1576.

[God] created Adam in his complete shape and form . . . sixty cubits (about 30 meters [90 feet]) in height.'"[6]

In some interpretations of the Islamic tradition, Adam and Eve were originally even taller, but Allah made them smaller. Islamic scholar Brannon Wheeler comments, "It is . . . reported that Adam was so tall that he could stand on the highest mountain . . . and see into

Jentil Giants

An unusual example of giants in religious myth is from the Basque region of Spain. The Basque people have a legend about a tribe of giants called the Jentil. Long ago they lived peacefully alongside humans. In some versions of the legend the giants were covered in hair and so tall that they could walk in the sea with their feet touching the bottom and their heads above water. According to the story, they always helped humans. For example, they invented metalworking and taught the Basque people to raise crops.

The legend of the Jentil giants changed over time, influenced by the teachings of Christian missionaries who started making their way across Europe around the late 300s. In a newer version of the legend, for instance, the giants flee to a hiding place beneath the earth when a bright star appears in the sky. The bright star that scared the giants, experts say, is taken from the New Testament story of the star that appeared in the sky at the moment of Jesus's birth.

Another example of Christianity's influence on the ancient legends of the Jentil giants is the story of Olentzero, said to be the last surviving giant. Today people in the Basque region honor Olentzero at Christmastime. It is said that he gives presents to all the children. In other words, Olentzero is the Basque version of Santa Claus.

heaven, so God reduced him to 60 cubits."[7] Ever since then Adam's descendants—that is, humans—have grown progressively shorter.

Hindu Legends of Giants

Hinduism, another of the world's major religions, also has many giants among its complex array of gods and supernatural beings. Notable among them are enormous supernatural beings called Daityas. They were the children of an earth goddess and a human wise man. These creatures were formed in the image of regular people but were colossal beings. They were so large that female Daityas wore jewelry the size of boulders.

Daityas were generally considered benevolent and friendly toward humans. However, they were not peaceful toward some of the other gods, just as the Titans of Greek legends had conflicts with other gods. Specifically, the Daityas fought their evil half brothers, the Devas, and opposed the practice of making sacrifices.

Another giant who figures in the Hindu religious tradition is a giant king named Muchukunda. His story is related in a religious epic, called the *Mahabharata*. Some of the gods favored Muchukunda, because the king had aided them in an especially fierce fight with other gods. As a reward, the gods granted Muchukunda any gift he desired. Joseph Campbell, a distinguished scholar of mythology, writes, "King Muchukunda, so runs the story, was very tired after his battle: all he asked was that he might be granted sleep without end, and that any person chancing to arouse him should be burned to a crisp by the first glance of his eye."[8]

According to this legend, the king slept for thousands of years, until another powerful king, Kalayavan, tried to invade Muchukunda's land. The god Krishna tricked Kalayavan into visiting the cave where Muchukunda was sleeping. Kalayavan kicked the sleeping giant. Campbell relates, "The [king] rose and the eyes that had been closed for unnumbered cycles of creation, world history, and dissolution, opened slowly to the light. The first glance that went forth struck the enemy king, who burst into a torch of flame and was reduced immediately to a smoking heap of ash."[9]

A Giant God in a Sumerian Religious Epic

Many other giants who were also gods (or were created by gods) appear in other religious legends. One notable example appears in a long poem from the ancient land of Sumer, in what is now part of Iraq. This poem is *The Epic of Gilgamesh*. Written on a dozen clay tablets, the poem is at least 2,000 years old. This makes it one of the world's oldest existing written stories.

The Epic of Gilgamesh describes the adventures of a king, Gilgamesh. One major section describes the king's encounter with a giant named Humbaba. Humbaba (or Huwawa) was a forest god who guarded a huge, sacred forest of cedar trees in a land that is now part of neighboring Iran. Humbaba was immensely old, and his appearance was terrifying and bizarre. According to some versions of the story, he had the face of a lion. In others, his face resembled the coiled intestines of an animal or a human.

King Gilgamesh wanted to travel to Humbaba's distant forest. As David Leeming, a scholar of mythology, relates, "Hating the sight of death and wishing to achieve fame and immortality, Gilgamesh, with his follower Endiku and with guidance from the sun god Utu, [set] out to fight Huwawa, the monstrous caretaker of the Cedar Forest."[10] The king also wanted to gather some of the valuable wood from the forest. (Gilgamesh's desert kingdom had no wood, so this was a valuable commodity.)

At first the king's friend and advisor Endiku told Gilgamesh not to go. He said of Humbaba, "His roaring is the flood-storm, his mouth is fire, his breath is death!"[11] But Gilgamesh was determined. He and Endiku gathered a small army and traveled to the edge of the forest. As they approached, they could hear Humbaba's terrifying roar. Endiku was worried for his king, but Gilgamesh decided to cut down some of the trees and battle the giant.

The noise of the king's army chopping down the trees alerted Humbaba, and the monster rushed to the spot. He threatened to kill the king, rip out his intestines, and feed his remains to the birds. The furious battle that followed shook the mountains around the forest. But Gilgamesh was victorious, defeating the giant god by thrusting a spear into his open mouth. The king was successful, according to the story, because the giant failed to wear more than one of the seven layers of his protective shield.

After the battle, Gilgamesh had been willing to show the monster mercy, but Endiku convinced him to cut the giant's head off. Then the two warriors and their army returned to Sumer by making a raft out of the wood they had gathered, and they floated home down the Euphrates River.

These and other stories about giants represent the many creation and religious myths and legends that have developed around the world. However, not all legends about gigantic humanlike creatures are associated with religion. Some are secular—that is, nonreligious.

Chapter 2

Giants in Folktales

As in creation and religious myths, giants are familiar figures in other folktales, legends, and fairy tales from around the world. As might be expected, the characteristics of these creatures vary considerably, depending on time and place.

In some cases there are many similarities, even in cultures that are separated by geography and time. For example, many giants are said to have red hair. On the whole, they differ widely. For example, some are associated with chaos, evil, and the unknown. Others, however, represent goodness and helpfulness.

Similarities Around the World

Not surprisingly, many legendary giants from around the world helped to explain powerful natural forces and specific land formations. For example, according to legend, Pele, the Hawaiian goddess of fire, lies underground and causes volcanic eruptions and earthquakes. Similar stories are told in Italy, where two volcanoes, Mount Etna and Mount Vesuvius, are said to be the burial places of giants who are still alive and breathing fire.

Still another legend explains the formation of remote islands off the rugged north coast of Iceland. According to this old story, two giants, a man and a woman, could come out only at night. Once, they were moving across the water, leading a cow. However, they did not finish crossing before dawn, and the sunlight changed them to stone. The cow is today the island of Drangey. Two smaller islands are what remain of the woman and man.

Cyclops

Another theme shared by many legends around the world is that clever people can defeat even the strongest giants. One famous example is the victory of David over Goliath. Cleverness also figures in ancient Greek stories about giants called the Cyclopes (the plural of Cyclops).

The most famous tale is in an epic by the Greek poet Homer. The hero Odysseus and his men were on a long sea voyage home when they encountered Polyphemos, a Cyclops who was the son of two gods. In the words of Pseudo-Apollodorus, a writer in ancient Greece, Polyphemos was "an enormous man-eating wild man . . . who had one eye in his forehead."[12]

Soon after the sailors arrived on the island where Polyphemos and the other cyclops lived, they sheltered in a cave. Polyphemos entered the cave, herding a flock of sheep in as well. He rolled a boulder across the entrance to keep them trapped there and then attacked Odysseus and some of his men. Homer described the terrible scene: "Then tearing them limb from limb he made his supper of them. He began to eat like a mountain lion, leaving nothing, devouring flesh and entrails and bones and marrow, while we in our tears and helplessness looked on at these monstrous doings and held up imploring hands to Zeus."[13]

But Odysseus tricked the Cyclops. He said that his name was Nobody. Then he gave the giant so much wine that he fell asleep. While the giant slumbered, Odysseus blinded him with a burning stake. Polyphemus cried out, but the other Cyclopes on the island ignored him because he shouted that "nobody" was to blame. Although in agony, Polyphemos rolled the stone away to let his sheep graze. Odysseus and the surviving crew escaped by clinging to the animals as they left.

Did You Know?

In Ethiopia, in northeast Africa, the Mensa people have a legend about a man who tried to steal cattle from a tribe of giants. One giant tried to kill the man, but another hid him in his massive cloak. The man was crushed when the two giants fought.

Some archaeologists have suggested that the legend of the Cyclopes was born when Greeks found the skulls of prehistoric dwarf elephants on the Mediterranean islands of Cyprus, Malta, Sicily, and Crete. These skulls were about twice as big as human skulls, each with a big cavity where the animals' trunks once were. These holes might have been mistaken for eye sockets.

The "Real" Jack and the Beanstalk

Greece's Cyclopes stories are only some of the European continent's rich traditions of colorful stories about giants. For some reason, they are especially abundant in Great Britain and Ireland.

Many giants from the British Isles were unusually stupid. One example comes from the town of Shrewsbury in England. A giant quarreled with the mayor and swore to walk to Shrewsbury and bury the town with dirt. But he met a cobbler who was carrying a load of used shoes. The shoemaker invented a story, telling the giant that he had worn out the shoes walking to Shrewsbury. The giant believed him and decided that traveling there would be too much work.

Legends from England, Ireland, Scotland, and Wales also feature giants who were responsible for the creation of ancient human-made structures. These stories tried to explain how such monuments came to be. One such structure is Stonehenge, a mysterious and massive grouping of stone slabs in the English countryside. According to a local legend, Stonehenge resulted from giants throwing boulders at each other.

But by far the most famous British giant is a creature called Cormoran. This giant is the star of a familiar fairy tale: "Jack and

The Fomorians of Ireland

Some people say that a race of enormous creatures called the Fomorians once existed in Ireland. (In some versions of the story, the Fomorians lived in Scotland.) It is believed that they may have been related to the ancient Greek Titans, which would mean that the Fomorians were half gods. The Fomorians were famous for their seafaring skills. Some scholars have translated their name from an old Irish phrase meaning "under the sea." So they may have originated as creatures who lived under the ocean.

Some ancient legends say that the Fomorians looked like humans but had heads like goats. In some versions of the story, they each had one eye, one leg, and one arm. Their leader was a ferocious monster named Balor who had an evil eye that would instantly freeze any human in terror. This eye was so large that it took 100 men to open the lid.

According to this story, the Fomorians demanded from the Irish people a yearly tax, so the people had to give the giants their crops and children. The Irish people resisted the tax for years, and after a series of bloody battles they finally succeeded in pushing the Fomorian giants off their island.

the Beanstalk." Although later said to live in the clouds, in the oldest tales about him Cormoran's home is a cave on a mountain rising from the sea off the rugged coastline of Cornwall in the southwest of England.

The giant was said to be 18 feet (5.49m) tall, with a waist 9 feet (2.74m) around. He was a fierce meat eater who periodically left his cave for the mainland, eating humans and livestock and collecting valuables such as gold coins salvaged from the many ships that wrecked off the rugged Cornish coast. When the residents of Cornwall offered this treasure as a reward for killing Cormoran, Jack, the son of a farmer, took up the challenge.

Jack swam to the island late one night and dug a deep pit. In the morning he loudly blew a horn. Furious at being wakened, Cormoran ran out, promising to broil the boy whole. But the giant fell into a pit, and Jack killed him with a sharp pickax. He took the giant's treasure as his reward and was known forevermore as Jack the Giant-Killer. According to legend, the giant was buried under a nearby rock formation that today is called the Giant's Grave. Local residents claim that a terrible groaning sound can sometimes be heard coming from under the formation.

Gog and Magog

A pair of brothers, Gog and Magog (called Gogmagog in some sources), are two other mythical giants from England. Stories about them are widespread and varied. They are mentioned in Judeo-Christian and Islamic religious texts, as well as in mythical tales from many other parts of the world.

> **Did You Know?**
>
> Today the Icelandic coat of arms features a rock giant who is one of the country's guardian spirits. He stood taller than the tallest mountain.

In an early version of the classic "Jack in the Beanstalk" tale, the giant falls into a pit and dies when Jack chops off his head. In later versions of this story, Jack chops down the beanstalk, which sends the giant crashing to the ground (as depicted in this 1917 illustration).

According to the British version of the legend, an emperor of Rome had 33 daughters. They murdered the men their father had chosen for them as husbands. To punish them the emperor set his daughters adrift in a boat, and they landed in England. There they mated with demons, and their children—including Gog and Magog—were giants. The wicked giants created havoc until they encountered Corineus, a hero from Cornwall. He killed Gog and Magog by throwing them into the sea from a high rock.

Gog and Magog have traditionally been the guardians of the City of London (now the heart of modern-day London). As such they are part of a common belief, in England and elsewhere, that giants are the protectors of certain towns and villages. Today London honors the brothers as part of a parade called the Lord Mayor's Show, which has been held every year since the mid-1500s. During this celebration huge, carved statues representing Gog and Magog are carried through the streets. In 1741 a writer named Thomas Boreman in his "Gigantick History" commented on their importance:

> Corineus and Gogmagog . . . richly valued their honour and exerted their whole strength and force in the defence of their liberty and country; so the City of London, by placing these, their representatives, in their Guildhall, emblematically declare, that they [Gog and Magog] will, like mighty giants defend the honour of their country and liberties of this their City; which excels all others, as much as those huge giants exceed in stature the common bulk of mankind.[14]

Legendary Irish Giants

Across the Irish Sea from the land where Gog and Magog lived, giants figure prominently in the mythology of Ireland. According to some sources, one of them was Crom Crumh Chomnaill, who spit fireballs from his enormous mouth. After terrorizing the Irish people for many years, the creature met his end when he encountered a Catholic saint.

According to a version of the legend, the saint's power was too strong for the monster. Writer Carol Rose notes, "Ultimately [the

The Pungalunga and the Mice Women

In Australia several tribes of aboriginal people near a place called Kata Tjuta ("Many Heads") have an ancient legend about creatures called the Pungalunga, who were cannibals and stood about 13 feet (3.96m) tall. These monsters hunted human beings for food and carried the bodies tucked into their belts. They had huge hands and powerful jaws so that they could easily catch and eat their prey.

In time all the Pungalunga died off except for one. One day he found an encampment of mice women and attacked them. But the mice women turned into wild dogs (the Australians call them dingoes) and chased him off. The giant ran until he found a tree. He pulled it from the ground and formed it into a boomerang, which he then used to smash out the teeth of the dogs. The toothless dogs then turned around and ran off.

In a place that is today Kata Tjuta National Park, a formation of about 40 huge, rounded rocks rises from the flat desert. The highest is about 1,500 feet (457.2m). They are thought to resemble the giant's bones and the mice women.

saint] managed to entice the monster into the river and trap him at the weir [dam]. There, the robes of the saint touched the evil Crom Crumh Chomnaill, who died immediately."[15]

But far and away the most famous of the Irish giants was not an enemy but a beloved hero. This was Finn McCool. According to legend, this mighty figure stood some 54 feet (16.46m) tall. Stories about this giant date from at least the third century AD. As with many folk figures, countless tales about him have sprung up over the centuries. One concerns the day a Scottish giant, Fingal, began shouting insults across the vast expanse of water between Scotland and Ireland. Finn retaliated by throwing giant heaps of earth into the sea, hoping to make a path across the channel so they could meet and fight.

Finn completed the job but was too exhausted to fight, so he devised another plan. He disguised himself as a baby, and when Fingal crossed the water, Finn's wife showed him her "son" sleeping in a cradle. Fingal was shocked—if the baby was so big, what would the father look like? The Scottish giant fled in terror back across the sea.

In another tale Finn threw a giant rock into the sea in an attempt to stop another enemy. This rock formed the Isle of Man, which today lies between England and Ireland.

There are many versions of how Finn died. The best known of these has him dying on the rugged Antrim coast, along Ireland's north shore. After his fatal fall from a cliff, Finn's feet became a rock formation that today is called the Giant's Causeway. This is a spectacular array of about 40,000 hexagonal columns, 36 feet (10.98m) high at their peak, that lead down to the sea. Meanwhile, his head formed a small island off the coast several miles to the east.

On the other hand, it is also said that Finn McCool is not dead at all. Instead, he is sleeping in a cave beneath the city of Dublin, waiting for a time when his country needs him.

Paul Bunyan

Rivaling Finn McCool and other famous European myths is North America's best-known legendary giant: Paul Bunyan. This massive lumberjack and his faithful companion, Babe the Blue Ox, are deeply embedded in America's folk traditions. However, the legend of Paul Bunyan is not nearly as old as European myths. In fact, it may be only about 200 years old. And its appearance in print is even more recent. The first time Paul Bunyan was mentioned in writing was in a 1906 newspaper article.

Dozens of stories have been told or written about America's best-known legendary giant, Paul Bunyan (pictured). The origins of the stories about the massive lumberjack are uncertain.

No one is sure where he came from. Some experts think that nineteenth-century lumberjacks invented him. Specifically, they may have modeled him on a French Canadian lumberjack, "Saginaw" Joe Fournier. The name *Bunyan*, meanwhile, may be a variation on *bony-enne*, a French Canadian slang word that can be roughly translated as "Good grief!"

There are dozens of stories about Paul Bunyan: It took five storks to carry him as a newborn. His father had to drive a horse and wagon hundreds of miles to rock the baby to sleep. When Paul learned to clap his hands, the vibrations were so strong that they broke every window in his parents' house. Paul Bunyan also showed early promise as a lumberjack. When he was not even a year old, he sawed the legs off his parents' bed.

As an adult the woodsman wandered far and wide to ply his trade. He was so strong that he carved out the Grand Canyon just by dragging his ax behind him. He dug out the Great Lakes to give Babe a proper watering hole. And while logging in Oregon, he built a cabin so big that its kitchen took up 10 square miles (25.9 sq. km).

Native American Legends

Paul Bunyan is hardly the only legendary giant in North America. Gigantic humanlike figures also appear in the myths of many Native American tribes. In the land of the Paiute Indians, in what is now Nevada, some people assert that men and women as tall as 12 feet (3.66m) lived there before and during the time of the Paiutes. These giants liked to eat humans, who finally ambushed the giants and killed most of them. The surviving giants hid in a cave and refused to come out and fight. The Paiutes then filled the cave with brush and set it on fire. Some of the giants ran out and were killed with arrows. Those who stayed choked to death on the smoke.

Another Native American legend is a story that the Ojibwa people tell about the Sleeping Giant, a landmark near Thunder Bay, Ontario in Canada. This rock formation is about 1,000 feet (304.8m) high and 7 miles (11.27km) long. It came into existence after the

Spirit of the Deep Water, Nanabijou, rewarded the people for their loyalty. He told them about a magnificent silver mine. The Ojibwa used the silver to make jewelry that became famous far and wide. Nanabijou warned that no one should tell white men about the mine. If this happened, the spirit would turn to stone. But a member of the Sioux tribe found the mine and told some white men. When these men tried to reach the mine, a storm came up and drowned them. After the storm cleared, the Ojibwa people saw that Nanabijou had indeed turned to stone. Today his body is the Sleeping Giant.

Giants of the South Pacific

Meanwhile, the native people of Hawaii have their own sleeping giant. This is a mountain ridge called Nounou on the island of Kauai. According to ancient legend, it was once a giant so large that the local people were able to plant broad fields of crops in his footprints.

One story says that the people got tired of the giant eating all their supplies, so they tricked him into eating rocks hidden in one of his meals. In another version he volunteered to build them a *heaiu*, a temple to the gods, and the task exhausted him. In both cases, the giant lay down to sleep on his back and never woke up. His body turned to rock and created the mountain range.

Also in the South Pacific, the island nation of Fiji has its own legends. One concerns a giant creature named Flaming Teeth. It is said that his teeth were as big and fiery as flaming logs. After the giant had terrorized the people for many years, the men managed to kill Flaming Teeth with a huge rock. However, his teeth continued to burn. The men took these teeth home, which gave the people fire for the first time.

South American Giants

As in North America and the Pacific Islands, South America also has many tales about giants. Early Spanish and English explorers

> ## Did You Know?
>
> According to one version of a legend of the Cocopah Indian tribe, who live in Arizona, ancient giants were so strong that they could carry logs that were too large for even six strong men.

recorded a number of these stories, and a surprising number of these Europeans reported personally seeing the giants. Among them were such well-known explorers as Amerigo Vespucci, Ferdinand Magellan, Hernando de Soto, and Sir Francis Drake.

An officer who accompanied the Portuguese explorer Magellan reported one such sighting in 1520. He recorded an encounter with aboriginal (native) people near the southern tip of South America. The officer wrote about one of them, "He was so tall that even the largest of us came only midway between his waist and his shoulder, yet withal [nonetheless] he was well proportioned."[16]

Of course, it is possible that the explorers saw nothing more than unusually tall humans. After all, the average size of Europeans was only about 5 feet 3 inches (1.6m) at the time, so unusually tall people may have looked like giants. On the other hand, maybe the explorers really did see genuine giants. In the sixteenth century, historian and writer Inca Garcilaso de la Vega recorded some of these stories.

De la Vega was of Spanish and Inca descent. His book *Royal Commentaries of the Incas* included stories he had heard as a child. One was about giants who had long ago come across the sea on huge rafts. He wrote:

[The giants] were so big that an ordinary man of good size scarcely reached up to their knees. . . . [It was] a monstrous thing to see their enormous heads and their hair hanging down about their shoulders. Their eyes were as large as small plates. They [the stories] say that they had no beards and that some of them were clad in the skins of animals, and others only in the dress nature gave them. . . .

When these great men or giants [made] their settlement . . . they destroyed and ate all the supplies they could find in the neighborhood. It is said that one of them ate more than fifty of the natives of the land; and as the supply of food was not sufficient for them to maintain themselves, they caught much fish with nets and gear that they had. They lived in continuous hostility with the natives.[17]

Giants Elsewhere

Across the Atlantic Ocean the native peoples of Africa also have dozens of legends about giants. For example, in West Africa, some cultures tell a traditional story that the world is actually the top of a giant's head. Plants and trees are the giant's hair, while animals and people are nothing more than insects crawling on his scalp. Earthquakes are the result of the giant sneezing or quickly turning his head.

Another legend, this one from the Khoikhoi people of South Africa, concerns a monstrous giant named Ga-Gorib. He stayed near a huge pit and challenged anyone passing by to throw a stone to knock him into the pit. The stone would bounce off the giant's huge belly and hit the thrower, who then fell in. This ended when a brave man tricked the giant. The man distracted him with conversation, then threw a stone that hit Ga-Gorib, who plunged to his death.

And in Asia, many cultures also have abundant legendary giants. For example, they figure prominently in Japan's rich heritage of stories about ghosts and supernatural creatures. One of the most famous of these tales concerns giant skeletons called *Gashadokuro*. According to Japanese folk tradition, Gashadokuro were terrifying creatures made of the bones and souls of people who had starved to death. They were immensely tall—some legends assert that they could be 90 feet (27.43m) high. Gashadokuro attacked humans at night if the people did not heed a warning sign: the faint sound of bells. When Gashadokuro caught humans, they bit off their heads—but the monsters' tremendous hunger was never satisfied.

One story about these creatures concerns a man who was in a field at night and heard a strange voice that complained about a

> ## Did You Know?
> An ancient legend from the Giant Mountains, on what is now the Czech Republic–Polish border, says that a giant named Rübezahl controlled the weather and had such a heavy step that he caused earthquakes when he walked.

painful eye. At daybreak, the man found an enormous skull. He took a cluster of bamboo shoots from the skull's eye and left a bowl of rice as an offering. This kindness caused the Gashadokuro to spare the man's life.

Stories about such legendary giants are so powerful that the tradition of telling them has survived well into present times. The creatures are so enduring, in fact, that they are embedded deep in today's popular culture.

Chapter 3

Giants in Popular Culture and the Arts

Giants have been portrayed in popular culture and the arts as both heroes and villains. They have appeared in movies, television shows, books, comic books and graphic novels, video games, and animated films. In some instances pop culture giants are simply new versions of old legends. The 2011 movie *Thor* features such creatures as the frost giants, who appear in Norse mythology. Giants have also found a place in recent entertainment, including many video and online games such as *Giant: Citizen Kabuto*.

Giants in pop culture come in many shapes, sizes, and personalities. Some are goofy and funny. Some are terrifying and dangerous. Some like the company of humans, while others are unfriendly. And some giants, willingly or not, alter their shapes and sizes.

No matter what form they take, giants continue to fascinate people and tickle their imaginations. Writer Joe Nickell comments, "Throughout literature, giants have provoked feelings of wonder and terror."[18]

Dreaded Movie Giants

The emphasis on terror and danger was particularly strong in many low-budget horror movies that date from the 1950s. They represented the fear of nuclear power that gripped the world during that time. As such, they symbolized a dread that science could go dangerously out of control.

Typically, the giant humans in these movies were created by radiation. The first major movie to depict this concept was *The Amazing Colossal Man*. In this film, released in 1957, an army officer is seriously burned by the blast of an atomic bomb. His wounds heal, but he grows into a bald, 60-foot (18.29m) monster. He also begins to go insane. The giant escapes from the hospital where he is being treated and destroys part of Las Vegas. However, military troops corner him at Hoover Dam, and he falls to his death.

Another well-known example of these movies is *Attack of the 50 Foot Woman*, released in 1958. It tells the story of a wealthy but troubled woman who is driving alone in the desert when she unexpectedly encounters a gigantic alien. She is exposed to radiation and grows to an astonishing height. She now has the power to take revenge on her deceitful husband and his new girlfriend. She is eventually killed when a power line falls on her, but not before she crushes her husband to death.

In 1993 *Attack of the 50 Foot Woman* was remade with actress Daryl Hannah. This new version used some of the same plot elements and themes. However, there was more emphasis on feminist power—and the giant woman does not die at the end.

Played for Laughs

The horror movies of the 1950s seem quaint by today's standards, and the special effects are crude. However, at the time they were meant to be genuinely frightening. At the other end of the scale,

> ## Did You Know?
>
> A movie from 1959, *The 30 Foot Bride of Candy Rock*, tells the story of a small-town amateur scientist whose girlfriend grows into a giant after swimming in mysterious hot springs.

ATTACK OF THE 50 FT. WOMAN

meanwhile, sometimes giants have been played strictly for laughs in the movies.

One example is the genuinely bizarre *Village of the Giants*, released in 1965. It combines elements of comedy, science fiction, and the then-popular beach-party movies. In it troublemaking teenagers discover a substance that makes them grow to enormous heights.

The teens take over a small town and force the adults to do their bidding. *Village of the Giants* is, by most standards, not a very good movie. However, it is notable for its cast. The film stars Beau Bridges (the brother of actor Jeff Bridges) as the leader of the gang. It also features a very young Ron Howard, another actor who would later become famous both for his acting and for directing movies.

There have since been many other comedies about humans who (at least temporarily) turn into giants. For instance, in *Honey, I Blew Up the Kid* (1992), a scientist invents a machine to make things grow. Things turn strange when he accidentally causes his two-year-old son to turn into a giant whenever he comes into contact with electricity.

Hercules, Goliath, and Cyclops

For a period in the 1950s and 1960s, movies about giants were especially popular with directors in Italy. Prominent among these movies were about 20 adventure stories loosely based on Hercules, a giant and immensely strong Roman warrior and half god. Among these movies, which were noted more for their lead actors' muscles than for any acting talent, were *Hercules vs. the Hydra*, *Hercules vs. the Sea Monster*, and *Hercules and the Captive Women*.

Several other adventure movies from that era featured giants. One was another Italian movie, *David and Goliath* (1961), which loosely retold the biblical story. It starred the famous American actor Orson Welles (as the king of the Jews) and an Italian muscleman (a circus star known only as Kronos) as Goliath. Italy also produced a series of adventure movies about a giant named Goliath (after the biblical character). These films played very freely with history and genres, as can be seen by their titles: *Goliath and the Masked Rider*, *Goliath and the Rebel Slave*, *Goliath and the Vampires*, *Goliath and the Dragon*, and *Goliath at the Conquest of Damascus*.

As might be expected, giants also figure in many other movies. One example is *The Cyclops*, from 1957. In it a woman searches in a remote part of Mexico for her fiancé, who has disappeared in a plane crash. When her own plane crashes, she and her companions land

Gargantua and Pantagruel

Giants are well represented in the classics of European literature. For example, two enormous creatures are major characters in an interconnected series of novels by François Rabelais, a famous French writer who lived in the fifteenth century. These satirical books were so outrageous, violent, and obscene that they were heavily censored in the author's time. The authorities felt that Rabelais was using his books to criticize religion and government.

Rabelais's giants are called Gargantua and Pantagruel. The creatures are father and son. Their size varies from chapter to chapter, according to the needs of the story. One section, for example, describes Pantagruel as an infant. He was so large that a cow nursed him—that is, until he ate the cow. In another section Pantagruel is so huge that a man lived in his mouth for six months, discovering in the process an entire society of people living around the giant's teeth. In another, Pantagruel is still a giant but is nonetheless small enough that he is able to fit into a human courtroom.

in a valley full of monstrous animals that have mutated because of radiation exposure. Among them is a ferocious 25-foot-tall (7.62m) human with a monstrous face and one eye.

Variations on this creature have appeared frequently, many of them only slightly related to the original Cyclops of ancient Greece. One example was a made-for-TV movie, *Cyclops* (2008). It starred Eric Roberts and placed the giant in ancient Rome, battling gladiators. Also, the character Cyclops in the X-Men movies has all of his power in his eyes. And a big-budget movie tentatively scheduled for release in 2014 will be based on a science-fiction graphic novel called *Cyclops*, about soldiers who wear single cameras in their helmets.

From Books to the Movies

Perhaps the best-known giant in the movies is Robbie Coltrane's portrayal of Rubeus Hagrid. Hagrid, as millions of fans know, is the kindhearted gamekeeper in J.K. Rowling's Harry Potter books. Hagrid's size changed in the transition from book to film: Rowling describes him as being 2 times as tall as an average man and 5 times as wide, but one of the movies specifies that he is 8 feet 6 inches (2.59m) tall.

Another famous fictional giant, the Hulk, began life in 1962 as a comic book star before moving to television and the movies. The Hulk was created when a human scientist, Bruce Banner, was exposed to radiation. The radiation caused Banner to lose control and

J.K. Rowling's beloved giant Hagrid (pictured here in a scene from the 2004 movie Harry Potter and the Prisoner of Azkaban*) is described in one of the books in the series as twice as tall and five times as wide as an average man.*

Dungeons and Dragons

Giants figure prominently in fantasy role-playing games. For example, giants appear often in *Dungeons and Dragons*, a pioneering fantasy role-playing game that has been extremely popular for years after its debut in 1974.

D&D, as it is often called, is played online or on a table. Like the online role-playing games that have become popular in recent years, the game has players taking on identities and forming groups to solve problems or to go on adventures in a fantasy world. Giants are important elements in the game. The official rulebook for *Dungeons and Dragons* has this to say about how giants act in the game:

> Giants combine great size with great strength, giving them an unparalleled ability to wreak destruction upon anyone or anything unfortunate enough to get in their way. . . .
>
> Giants have a reputation for crudeness and stupidity that is not undeserved, especially among the evil varieties. Most rely on their tremendous strength to solve problems, reasoning that any difficulty that won't succumb to brute force isn't worth worrying about. Giants usually subsist by hunting and raiding, taking what they like from creatures weaker than themselves.

Wizards of the Coast, "Giants," *Dungeons & Dragons Monster Manual*. Renton, WA: Wizards of the Coast, 2003, p. 119.

transform, against his will, into a green and phenomenally strong giant whenever he became extremely angry.

The Hulk TV series, starring Bill Bixby as Dr. Banner, ran from 1978 to 1982. One of the actors who auditioned to play the giant was Arnold Schwarzenegger. At the time, he was a professional

The Hulk *television series, which ran from 1978 to 1982, featured Lou Ferrigno (pictured) as the massively muscled, green-colored giant who was created as a result of accidental exposure to radiation.*

bodybuilder just breaking into acting. However, the part went to another strongman, Lou Ferrigno.

In 2003 the first movie about the Hulk was released. It starred Eric Bana as Bruce Banner. The second film was released in 2008, with Edward Norton taking the lead role. The two films had very different plotlines. In the first movie Banner experiments on himself, trying to make human DNA better, while in the second film he is exposed to radiation during military experiments to create a super-soldier.

Another movie that was based on a comic book hero (who was in turn based loosely on ancient Norse legends) was *Thor*. In the 2011 movie Thor and his father, Odin, battle the fierce frost giant Laufey and his warriors. The actors who played the frost giants spent three to four hours every day in makeup and costuming in preparation for their roles.

TV and Commercials

In addition to starring in movies for decades, giants have also been featured on TV. For example, the series *Land of the Giants* ran for two seasons from 1968 to 1970. Its plotline involved astronauts who were forced to go off course and land on a planet where everything was huge—including humanlike giants standing about 70 feet (21.34m) tall.

Television has also been a popular venue for commercials and ad campaigns involving giants. Far and away the most famous of these is the Jolly Green Giant, who began life in 1928. Today this figure is one of the most recognized advertising icons in the world and still stars in commercials for the Green Giant Company, which makes frozen and canned vegetables. In Blue Earth, Minnesota, a 55-foot (16.76m) statue of the Jolly Green Giant advertises the fact that the Green Giant vegetable company is located nearby.

Another example of a TV ad was produced in 2003 for an Italian sports gear company, Puma. In this commercial a beautiful model plays a giantess who crashes through a city, Godzilla-like, destroying buildings and eating a man. (She tips her head back and swallows him whole.) However, a handsome athlete throws a ball at her to attract her attention. He catches her eye, and she bends over to kiss him, ending her destructive rampage.

Comic Books and Graphic Novels

Giants have also been staples of comic books for decades. In addition to the Hulk, there have been many others. One of the most popular has been the Avengers series, featuring the character Giant Man. Giant Man, who debuted in 1962, was the alter ego of Hank Pym, a brilliant scientist who found a way to alter the molecular structure of objects, thus giving him the ability to change size at will (and to mentally cause changes in objects as well). Pym's adventures continue to this day, although his character has undergone several changes, including transformations into Ant-Man, Goliath, Yellowjacket, and the Wasp.

In comic books, graphic novels, and elsewhere, the majority of giants are male. Not all of them are men, however. One example appears in Wonder Woman, a series of comic books with a long life—the series began in 1944 and is still going strong. A recurring character is Giganta, an evil, red-haired villain who can change her size at will.

Giants also figure in some graphic novels, which are hybrids of fiction and comic books. One such book is *3 Story: The Secret History of the Giant Man*, which appeared in 2009. Its author, Matt Kindt, tells the story of Craig Pressgang, a man who keeps growing and finds it increasingly impossible to live comfortably or happily in the normal-sized world.

Anime, Manga, and Video Games

Anime may have even more colorful and inventively imagined giants than comic books do. Anime are animated films from Japan. They usually stress adventure, romance, and humor, typically with a supernatural or fantasy background. Related to them are manga, Japanese comic books with similar themes. The themes of anime and manga frequently overlap with each other and with a third form of entertainment: video games.

Many of the giants in anime, manga, and games are essentially oversized but humanoid robots. Game journalist Arlen Pringle comments, "A staggering amount of anime has giant robots in it."[19] One notable example is in *FLCL* (*Fooly Cooly*), which features giant battling robots that emerge from the head of a teenager—just one of many eerie but funny events surrounding a futuristic factory in the boy's town. Like many manga and anime shows, *FLCL* mixes crazy humor into its adventure and fantasy.

On the other hand, many anime giants are not robots but are genuine and oversized humans. One of the best known is in *Dragon Ball*, a pioneering and wildly popular manga and anime series that began in 1984. Based on ancient Japanese and Chinese folk legends, it tells the story of Goku, a martial arts expert (originally from an-

> ## Did You Know?
>
> One of the many giants starring in manga is Mana Eimiya, a 160-foot (48.78m) girl devoted to battling invading aliens. She also happens to be in love with a normal-sized human boy.

other planet) who wanders the world looking for mystical objects called Dragon Balls.

One character in *Dragon Ball* is Goku's father-in-law, the giant known as Ox-King. The Ox-King rules a region called Fire Mountain. His looks change quite a bit as the series progresses. For example, early in the series he has a huge beard, wears a helmet with goggles, and carries an ax. Later in the series he looks more conventional. Similarly, early on he is fierce and eats people and animals who come too close to Fire Mountain. Later, however, he is gentle, fun loving, and devoted to keeping his daughter Chi-Chi, Goku's wife, away from danger and out of trouble.

More Manga

Another example of a manga giant is Vice Admiral John Giant from the series *One Piece*. This series is about a boy with magical elastic powers who travels the world looking for the ultimate treasure, which will make him the Pirate King. John Giant, as his name and rank imply, is a fierce, sword-wielding naval officer several times taller and stronger than average.

A very different kind of giant is the character called Granmamare, in a hit 2008 anime film called *Ponyo*. The movie was written and directed by a gifted artist, Hayao Miyazaki. Ponyo is a goldfish that wants to become a human girl. Granmamare is her mother, a magical creature who looks like a giant human woman swimming in the ocean. *Time* magazine writer Richard Corliss, in a review of the movie, compared Granmamare to a glamorous character in a film style in India called Bollywood. Corliss commented that Granmamare is "a magnificent sea goddess, with the perfect posture and forehead jewel of a Bollywood queen."[20]

Video Games

As for games that feature giants, one popular and critically praised example is *Shadow of the Colossus*. The player, acting as a human named Wander, travels across a strange, stark land on a horse. He must defeat a series of giants, each with different strengths and weaknesses, using only a sword, a bow, and his horse. The giants he battles are called Colossi, a reference to the Colossus of Rhodes, an enormous statue in ancient Greece.

In the game the Colossi are heavily armed creatures. Each one is different. For example, each has control over a certain territory, and each has individual traits (such as being aggressive, attacking only when attacked, or being completely passive). Furthermore, their bodies are made up of many kinds of things, such as rock and flesh, that do not exist together in real life. Some of the Colossi look human, others like animals. Some live in the water and some on land or in the air.

Pringle, the game journalist, says that *Shadow of the Colossus* is unusual and notable for several reasons. For one thing, he says players are told almost nothing at the start of the game—the game had a mysterious quality that forced players to think about what they are doing. Pringle comments:

> [The] time you spend exploring the landscape, the general silence, and the actions of the Colossi themselves make you doubt why you're doing any of this in the first place. . . . The scale of the game is also very impressive, as no game had ever done giants as well in terms of sound and scale. [And] it didn't talk down to you or badger you with dialog. The game let you come to your own conclusions.[21]

Giants in Books and Literature

For hundreds of years before the advent of anime, manga, and games, giants have been prominent figures in novels and other writings—sometimes terrifying and sometimes friendly. Among the many giants who figure in literature are the Efts, 14-foot (4.27m) creatures resembling trees, in J.R.R. Tolkien's *The Hobbit*. Other instances include Roald Dahl's *The BFG* (Big Friendly Giant) and, of course, Hagrid in the Harry Potter books.

And giants roam all over the fairy tales collected by the Grimm brothers. One is the enormous creature in "The Young Giant," a gentle creature who adopts a tiny boy and nurtures him until he, too, becomes a giant. Others include the giant in "The Giant and the Tailor" (The giant is not overly friendly—or bright, for that matter). And "The Skillful Huntsman" features not one but three wicked giants.

Meanwhile, a character in *The Tin Woodman of Oz*, one of L. Frank Baum's many books about Oz, is Mrs. Yoop, an immense female giant, or giantess, who welcomes the book's main characters to Yoop Castle. Baum noted that she was amiable and wore "silver robes embroidered with gay floral designs, and . . . a short apron of elaborate lace-work."[22]

Giants figure in many other classics of literature as well. For instance, in Jonathan Swift's satirical fantasy *Gulliver's Travels*, published in 1726, Swift's wandering hero encounters the Brobdignagians, a race of giants described variously as 72 feet (21.95m) or 60 feet (18.29m) tall.

Did You Know?

In the classic children's book *Alice in Wonderland* by Lewis Carroll, Alice drinks a potion that temporarily turns her into a giant.

Paul Bunyan in Statue and Birthplace

Legendary giants also stride through areas of popular culture outside the realm of literature. North America's most famous contribution to giants in pop culture, Paul Bunyan, is the center of much of this activity.

Many towns in North America claim to be the woodsman's birthplace or burial spot. Bangor, Maine; Akeley, Minnesota; and Bemidji, Minnesota, are just three of his alleged birthplaces. Meanwhile, Rib Mountain, near Wausau, Wisconsin, and Kelliher, Minnesota, are just two of the locations where he is allegedly buried.

By far, Bunyan is also the most popular subject for America's ongoing love affair with giant statues. Some of these enormous monuments advertise businesses. But many cities and towns have erected them to bolster their claims to be his birthplace. One such town is Oscoda, Michigan, where the local newspaper published in 1906 the first documented stories about the woodsman. Oscoda's statue honoring Bunyan is about 25 feet (7.62m) high. But it is by no means the only one. Among the many other towns that have statues honoring the woodsman are Bemidji, Minnesota; Brainerd, Minnesota; Shelton, Washington; Westwood, California; Bay City, Michigan; Wahoo, Nebraska; Alpena, Michigan; Eau Claire, Wisconsin; and Bangor, Maine. Furthermore, many festivals around the country honor the giant logger. These include celebrations in Fort Bragg, California; St. Maries, Idaho; Akeley, Minnesota; and Oscoda, Michigan.

The Cerne Abbas Giant

A much older example of a giant figure in "real life" can be seen outside the United States. It is near Cerne Abbas, a small village in southwest England. There the image of a naked giant holding a club is cut into the side of a steep hill. This carving, called the Cerne Giant, is 180 feet (54.86m) long and 167 feet (50.9m) wide. Because there is chalk underneath the hill's grass and earth, the giant looks white when seen from a distance or from the air.

According to tradition, the figure represents a legendary giant, although its significance is unknown. Legend has it that the giant lived sometime before 1000 AD. However, the year the carving was made is unknown, and it is almost certainly much more recent than 1000 AD. British journalist Petronella Wyatt writes:

> Some say he is a pagan fertility symbol and that if a childless woman and her partner spend the night camping between the giant's legs, she will be a mother within two years.
>
> Others claim that the figure represents the [Roman] hero Hercules, who was often depicted with a club in his right hand. Either way, there are no documents mentioning the giant before 1694.[23]

The Cerne Giant has been the target of numerous pranks over the years, including an instance when it was temporarily painted purple. It has also figured in an advertising campaign. In 2007, to advertise the British opening of *The Simpsons Movie*, a giant image of Homer Simpson holding a doughnut was painted next to the giant. However, this image did not last long. Since it was made with water-based, biodegradable paint, Homer was soon washed away by rain.

Invention or Real?

Serious scholars of the subject agree that all of the giants portrayed in popular culture, like the enormous creatures in ancient legends and myths, are inventions. They feel the same way about the accounts of giants that are still regularly reported.

However, many people believe that these reports have at least some degree of truth. They assert that giants really did roam the earth once upon a time and may still do so.

Chapter 4

Modern Times: Giants Both Alleged and Real

Reports of giants continue to pop up the world over. These reports are sometimes put forward as truth. People with an interest in unexplained mysteries or who want to study religious references to giants are the source of much of this speculation. However, such accounts typically stem from unconfirmed rumors, misunderstandings, theories, or outright hoaxes.

The ease of communicating through the Internet has created an explosion in the amount of this speculation, since the net makes new webs among interested people easy to create. Sometimes the speculation about giants leads to conspiracy theories. These theories seek to show that scientists and government officials are covering up proof that ancient giants really existed—and that more modern ones also exist.

Giants in the Old West

For some reason, most reports of giants that allegedly existed in the last two centuries come from North America. Many come from the American Southwest, a region that includes Texas, New Mexico, Arizona, Nevada, and the desert territory of Southern California. They often date from the nineteenth century, when these regions still made up the Old West.

One of these stories concerns an incident in 1833 in Lompock Rancho, California. Allegedly, a group of Mexican soldiers was digging a pit for storing ammunition when they unearthed a skeleton. In the book *Weird California*, the authors write, "Not unusual, except that this skeleton . . . was twelve feet tall."[24]

In addition to its extraordinary height, this giant also apparently had double rows of teeth, on both the top and bottom. Furthermore, the skeleton was allegedly surrounded by objects such as stone axes and shells that might have been burial offerings. This could indicate that the skeleton was that of an important person and that these objects were meant to help it in the next life. Proof of a genuine giant find in Lompock Rancho in the 1800s has never surfaced.

Unconfirmed reports of real giants have surfaced in various parts of North America, including the Grand Canyon (pictured), where, in 1923, an explorer claimed to have found the petrified human remains of two giants: one 15 feet tall and the other 18 feet tall.

Buffalo Bill and the Giants

A report of bones that came from a legendary giant in the Old West was reported in the autobiography of the famous figure William "Buffalo Bill" Cody. This book, first published in 1879, refers to a Pawnee Indian legend. Cody (who was well known for exaggerating or inventing colorful stories) noted an incident in a region that now covers parts of Colorado, Wyoming, Kansas, and Nebraska. He wrote:

> While we were in the sandhills, scouting the Niobrara country, the Pawnee Indians brought into camp some very large bones, one of which the surgeon of the expedition pronounced to be the thigh bone of a human being. The Indians said the bones were those of a race of people who long ago had lived in that country.
>
> They said these people were three times the size of a man of the present day, that they were so swift and strong that they could run by the side of a buffalo and, taking the animal in one arm, could tear off a leg and eat it as they ran.

William F. Cody, *An Autobiography of Buffalo Bill*. Rockville, MD: Phoenix Rider, 2009, p. 117.

More North American Giants

In the 1880s, meanwhile, 7-foot (2.13m) human skeletons were allegedly unearthed near Sayre, in Bradford County, Pennsylvania. The skulls supposedly had horns about 2 inches (5.08cm) above their eye sockets. According to one version of this tale, the people who found the remains, two professors and a Pennsylvania state historian, donated their find to a museum in Philadelphia, but the remains were later lost or stolen.

During this same period, archaeologists explored an ancient burial mound near Brewersville, Indiana, and allegedly found a human skeleton measuring 9 feet 8 inches (2.95m). The skeleton wore a necklace made of a rock called mica. However, it was also reported that these bones disappeared in a flood in 1937. The disappearance of these and the Bradford County bones has been the cause of considerable speculation over the years that the incidents have, for mysterious reasons, been covered up.

Allegedly, the remains of numerous other giants have been discovered in North America. For example, it was reported that in 1923 a man named Samuel Hubbard, exploring in the Grand Canyon, found two petrified humans, respectively 15 feet (4.57m) and 18 feet (5.49m) tall. Meanwhile, another canyon, Barranca del Cobre (Copper Canyon) in the Mexican state of Chihuahua, was the location where an explorer, Paxton Hayes, allegedly found 34 mummified men and women, all between 7 and 8 feet (2.13m and 2.44m) in height.

And in 1947 the *San Diego Union* newspaper reported that the mummified remains of 80,000-year-old giants were supposedly discovered in caves in the Nevada-California desert. Allegedly, these mummies were clothed in jackets and pants made from the wool of an unidentified animal.

> **Did You Know?**
> Workers digging the foundation of a new building in 1891 in Crittenden, Arizona, allegedly found a huge stone coffin containing the bones of a 9-foot-tall (2.74m) giant.

Red-Haired Giants and More

A surprising number of reports of skeletons or the mummified remains of giants mention mysterious red-haired creatures who lived long before humans arrived on the earth. Reports concerning these redheaded giants have come from such geographically distant areas as Ireland, the deserts of northwest China, Hawaii, and the American Southwest.

Although they differ somewhat, most of these stories have certain things in common. Aside from having reddish hair, the remains have typically been found in ancient burial mounds, indicating that they did not die alone but were instead members of tribes that buried them. And generally they were found 9 to 12 feet (2.74m to 3.66m) under the surface of the burial mound. Furthermore, their grave sites often included objects scattered around that were meant to help them in the next life.

A typical example of an alleged red-haired giant comes from the American Southwest and dates from the early twentieth century. In 1911 a team of workers started clearing a layer of bat guano several feet thick from Lovelock Cave near Lovelock, Nevada. (Guano is excrement that has long been used in making fertilizer and gunpowder.) Under the guano were allegedly several mummified human bodies, all over 7 feet (2.13m) tall, with their reddish hair still intact.

Although not necessarily redheaded, skeletal remains of giants have reportedly been found in many other places around the world. Among the countries where people claim to have uncovered enormous skeletons are Israel, India, and Saudi Arabia.

One intriguing discovery was apparently made in 2010 in the South Pacific island nation of Fiji. This discovery is a fossilized human footprint some 13 inches (33.02cm) long and 8 inches (20.32cm) wide. The size of this footprint indicates that whoever made it was about 6 feet 6 inches (1.98m) tall—much taller than the average Fijian today. The field research officer of the Fiji Museum, Sepeti Matararaba, told a reporter, "We are inviting people to come and see the size of the people that lived in Fiji in early days; they were huge when compared to people living nowadays, especially when we see the size of the footprint on the stone."[25]

The Cardiff Giant

While the truth and accuracy of such reports may be debated, some descriptions of ancient giants are just plain wrong. This is especially so in the case of hoaxes—tricks that are played to fool people into believing something.

The most famous hoax, involving an apparently ancient giant, was the case of the Cardiff Giant. This amazing swindle captured the public imagination for years—and remained popular long after it had been exposed as phony. The Cardiff Giant was "born" in 1868. It was the brainchild of George Hull, a cigar manufacturer in New York State. Hull apparently had several reasons for coming up with the idea. One was to make a profit (by charging admission to see it). Another was a desire to make mischief: Hull, an atheist, wanted to make fun of people who took literally the Bible's claim that giants once walked the earth.

Hull hired sculptors to carve in secret a 10-foot-tall (3.05m), 3-ton (2.72-metric-ton) giant out of a soft rock called gypsum. After Hull's workmen scoured the carving with sulfuric acid and dug holes in it to make it look old, he had it buried on a relative's farm near the town of Cardiff, New York. A year later, in 1869, workers hired to dig a well on the farm "accidentally" found the alleged petrified man.

It was the source of great controversy, with some people fiercely defending the discovery as genuine, while others claimed it was an ancient statue—and still others asserting that it was nothing more than a fake. No matter: Hull made a fortune from the Cardiff Giant by collecting 50 cents from each of the thousands of visitors who wanted a peek at it. He then sold it to a group of businessmen—for another large sum of money—and they sent it on tour.

Not to be outdone, the king of showmanship, P.T. Barnum, commissioned a replica of the Cardiff Giant—in other words, a fake of a fake. Barnum, a genius at publicizing himself and his shows, offered a reward of $1,000 to anyone who could prove his giant was more legitimate than the original. Barnum's giant toured the country during the late 1860s in one of his traveling shows, and both versions were revealed as phony in 1870, when the two were exhibited in New York City at the same time. At that point, Hull admitted that his creation was a fake.

The original Cardiff Giant is still on display, in a museum in Cooperstown, New York. To explain its enduring appeal, Alex Boese, curator of the Museum of Hoaxes, commented, "Many have declared the Cardiff Giant to be the greatest hoax of all time. Whether or not this is the case, its huge size and mysterious presence certainly tapped into some strange element of the . . . American psyche."[26]

> **Did You Know?**
>
> The pituitary gland, the part of the brain that controls height, is only the size of a pea.

Gigantism

The Cardiff Giant and virtually all other reports of giants through-out the centuries are based on little more than legend, hearsay, religious belief, speculation, or sheer invention. However, there are genuine giants who have clearly and demonstratively lived—and who live today. These giants are by no means monsters or terrifying creatures. They are certainly not to be feared or gawked at. They are, indeed, just human beings who happen to be abnormally tall as the result of a medical condition. Márta Korbonits, in London, comments, "These people are not weirdos or freaks, but just ordinary ill people [who should be regarded] as many of us [are who have] . . . other diseases, such as heart disease or diabetes."[27]

Their medical condition is called gigantism. Gigantism results from an excess of growth hormone. This abnormality is typically caused by a tumor that affects a tiny part of the brain, called the pituitary gland, that controls the growth hormone. Sometimes surgery, radiation therapy, or medication can stop or control the condition, but often it resists treatment.

Typically, people with gigantism suffer from a variety of serious health conditions. Their enormous size places strains on their bodies, resulting in problems such as weakened hearts, diabetes, breathing difficulties, and limited muscle and bone functions. Because of their health problems, people with gigantism usually must use canes or wheelchairs to move, are in constant pain, and die at a relatively young age.

Gigantism is very rare. Daniel Kelley, the medical director of the Neuro-Endocrine Tumor Center at Saint John's Health Center in Santa Monica, California, comments, "About one in 20 people will have an abnormality in their pituitary gland [but] based on some recent demographic studies, [only] about one in 1,000 people probably have a symptomatic pituitary adenoma [the tumor that causes gigantism]."[28]

> **Did You Know?**
>
> Andre the Giant, a well-known wrestler and actor in the 1970s and 1980s, was described in publicity materials as 7 feet 4 inches (2.24m) tall, although that height may be a bit of a stretch.

Real Irish Giants

For reasons that are not clear, Ireland produces a larger-than-normal number of people with gigantism. This may account for some of the stories about legendary giants of old, since the genetic makeup that causes the condition is passed from one generation to the next.

One such case has already been proved through DNA analysis. In 2011 an international team of scientists examined the bones and teeth of one of Ireland's most famous giants. This was Charles Byrne, who lived in the seventeenth century. He was 7 feet 7 inches (2.31m) tall. Although he wished to be buried at sea to avoid doctors examining his body, Byrne's skeleton was saved after his death and today is on display at the Royal College of Surgeons in London, England. This was the skeleton that the scientific team examined in 2011.

They found something very interesting. The team discovered a genetic link connecting Byrne with four families in Northern Ireland. These families' many branches still thrive. Meanwhile, the same genetic trait links Byrne and his descendants with their ancient ancestors, dating back at least 1,500 years. This means that some of Ireland's legendary giants likely had gigantism—and were the direct ancestors of people living today.

Of the related people today, an estimated 200 to 300 of them have inherited the mutated gene that caused Byrne's condition. One of these people is Brendan Holland, who is 6 feet 9 inches (2.06m) tall. As a teenager Holland grew abnormally tall and became less coordinated. He experienced frequent violent headaches and occasional episodes of blindness. However, when he was 20, Holland's tumor was found and treated with radiotherapy. His headaches and attacks of blindness disappeared, and his growth hormone levels dropped to normal.

Not surprisingly, Holland is grateful that his condition could be treated. He commented to a reporter, "I consider myself extraordinarily lucky. I know that my children or my grandchildren could be screened for this rogue gene and if they are sufferers . . . they can be given early treatment."[29]

Sideshows and Carnivals

People with gigantism, like Holland, are clearly not freakish or scary monsters. However, until recently they were often treated as social outcasts. These huge individuals found it difficult to find regular work. As a result, many of them were forced to join circuses or other shows where they were displayed as freaks of nature. One example was a young Englishman who stood at 7 feet 4 inches (2.24m). He appeared onstage in the mid-1700s, balancing on a tightrope and performing other tricks.

An advertisement for his show drew comparisons between him and the ancient legendary giants of England. It read, in part, "The

The Potsdam Giants

Historically, people with gigantism have found it difficult to find regular jobs. On occasion, they could find work as soldiers. The most famous of these giant soldiers belonged to a special regiment of enormous military men in the seventeenth and eighteenth centuries. These were the Potsdam Giants, named for the city in Prussia (now part of Germany) where they were stationed.

The minimum height for this elite regiment was set at 6 feet 2 inches (1.88m). This was enormously tall for the time. By contrast, King Frederick William I of what was then Prussia, who founded the regiment, was only about 5 feet 2 inches (1.57m) tall.

Frederick was apparently so determined to enlist increasingly large numbers of Potsdam soldiers that he paid farmers to enlist their tall sons, arranged marriages between unusually tall men and women, and sometimes resorted to kidnapping if candidates resisted. The English writer Thomas Carlyle noted of this unusual group of soldiers that they were "a mass of shining giants . . . and the shortest man of them rises, I think, towards seven feet [2.13m] [while] some are nearly nine feet high [2.74m]. Men from all countries; a hundred and odd come annually, as we saw, from Russia. . . . The rest have been [recruited] out of every European country, at enormous expense, not to speak of other trouble to his majesty."

Charles DeLoach, *Giants*. Metuchen, NJ: Scarecrow, 1995, p. 238.

greatest . . . can now be shown in every evening . . . a young Colossus, who, though not 16, . . . has drawn more company this season than was ever known before, and must convince the world that the ancient race of Britons is not extinct, but that we may yet hope to see a race of giant-like heroes."[30]

Two other giants who performed in public were Anna Swan, who stood at 7 feet 5 inches (2.26m), and Martin Bates, who was 7 feet 2 inches (2.18m) tall. Both of them were part of P.T. Barnum's circus and museum shows. They traveled extensively, including a tour of Europe, and when the two married in England in 1871, the bride wore a dress and jewelry given to her by England's Queen Victoria.

After history's tallest known couple retired, they lived on a farm in Ohio in a specially built house, with 8-and-a-half foot (2.6m) doorways and other custom-built features. The local church had a special pew built for them. After his wife died in 1888, Bates married the daughter of the church's pastor. She was just over 5 feet (1.52m) tall.

The practice of appearing in circuses and other venues has persisted into modern times. For example, Sandra Allen, who was 7 feet 7 inches (2.31m) tall, spent some of her life touring with the Ringling Brothers Circus and was a frequent guest on television talk shows before her death in 2008.

Tallest Man Ever

Another person who toured with circuses and other forms of entertainment was Robert Pershing Wadlow of Alton, Illinois. Wadlow was an astonishing 8 feet 11 inches (2.72m) tall, making him the tallest documented human in history.

Wadlow was born in 1918. He had normal weight as a newborn, but he grew at an alarming rate. By 6 months, he weighed 30 pounds (13.6kg), and more than double that a year later. He reached 6 feet 2 inches (1.88m) and 195 pounds (88.45kg) by the time he was 8 years old—big enough to carry his father up the stairs.

Wadlow had normal-sized parents and four normal-sized siblings, and as a young man he tried to lead as ordinary a life as possible. For example, he collected stamps and matchbooks, and he took up photography. He even became a Boy Scout at the age of 13—by which time he was 7 feet 4 inches (2.24m) tall.

As an adult, Wadlow attended college, but being a student proved to be nearly impossible for him. His hands were too large to handle items such as pens, pencils, notebooks, and lab equipment. Nor could he walk on campus in Illinois's icy winter conditions, since a fall would shatter his brittle bones. He had to quit after a year. His clothes required three times the normal amount of cloth. On the other hand, his custom-made size 37AA shoes were provided free by a shoe company in exchange for publicity.

As it happened, Wadlow's enormous feet were the immediate cause of his death. He had never had much feeling in them, so he did not notice a blister that formed after a leg brace chafed him. The blister became infected, which in the days before the widespread use of antibiotics was very serious. Despite emergency surgery, Wadlow died at the age of 22.

At the time of his death Wadlow weighed 490 pounds (222.26 kg), and 20 pallbearers were needed to carry his custom-made, half-ton coffin to the grave. Many businesses in Alton closed for his funeral, and an estimated 40,000 people attended. Today the town of Alton has honored him with a life-size statue.

The Tallest People Today

In the years since Wadlow's death, no one has come close to his record. Currently, the tallest person in the world is a Turkish farmer, Sultan Kösen. He stands 8 feet 1 inch (2.46m) high. The tallest woman alive, at 7 feet 8 inches (2.34m), is Yao Defen of China. Unfortunately, like so many people with gigantism, Kösen and Yao have a variety of health problems associated with their condition.

Some people who are extremely tall do not have gigantism—they are just very tall. For example, the Tutsi people of central Africa have a reputation for being extremely tall. However, statistics on the Tutsis vary widely. Some sources say that Tutsi men average only 5 feet 7 inches (1.7m), while others claim that they average nearly 7 feet (2.13m).

Perhaps the best-known tall people today are basketball stars. One of them was Manute Bol, who stood 7 feet 6 inches (2.29m) and played for a number of National Basketball Association teams before his death from a rare skin disease in March 2011 at the age of 47. Two other basketball greats are Gheorghe Muresan (7 feet 7 inches, or 2.31m), now retired after a career with the Washington Bullets, and Yao Ming (7 feet 6 inches, or 2.29m) of the Houston Rockets.

However, not even the towering Yao is the tallest basketball player in the world. Sun Mingming (7 feet 9 inches, or 2.36m) plays for a pro team in China. He wears size 20 shoes. Unlike other basketball players, Sun does have gigantism. He had a tumor on his pituitary gland, but it was successfully treated, and he has been able to continue playing professionally.

Many people today believe that stories of giants are nothing more than that—just stories that were invented to explain the creation of the world or natural phenomena. However, other people contend that these legendary giants were indeed real at one time. They ask: Did giants really once stride across the earth? Perhaps the truth will never be known. In the meantime, legendary and mythical giants remain fascinating and elusive subjects for exploration and thought.

Source Notes

Introduction: Giants Roam the Earth

1. Carol Rose, *Giants, Monsters, and Dragons*. Santa Barbara: ABC-CLIO, 2000, p. xxv.

Chapter One: Creation Myths and Religious Legends

2. Statius, *The Thebaid*, Theoi Project. www.theoi.com.
3. Snorri Sturluson, "Skáldskaparmal," Internet Sacred Text Archive. www.sacred-texts.com.
4. Genesis 6:4–5, King James Version. Official King James Bible Online, 2011. www.kingjamesbibleonline.org.
5. Numbers 13:33, King James Version. Biblos.com. http://bible.cc.
6. *Sahih al-Bukhari*, "Asking Permission," Center for Muslim-Jewish Engagement, University of Southern California. www.usc.edu.
7. Quoted in Oliver Leaman, ed., *The Qur'an: An Encyclopedia*. New York: Routledge, 2006, p. 11.
8. Joseph Campbell, *The Hero with a Thousand Faces*. Novato, CA: New World Library, 2008, p. 168.
9. Campbell, *The Hero with a Thousand Faces*, p. 168.
10. David Leeming, *Jealous Gods, Chosen People*. New York: Oxford University Press, 2004, p. 56.
11. Quoted in Paul Ricoeur, *The Symbolism of Evil*. Boston: Beacon, 1986, p. 188.

Chapter Two: Giants in Folktales

12. Pseudo-Apollodorus, *Bibliotheca*, Theoi Project. www.theoi.com.
13. Homer, *The Odyssey*, Theoi Project. www.theoi.com.

14. Quoted in Lord Mayor's Show 2011, "Gog and Magog," 2011. www.lordmayorsshow.org.

15. Rose, *Giants, Monsters, and Dragons*, pp. 88–89.

16. Quoted in Charles DeLoach, *Giants*. Metuchen, NJ: Scarecrow, 1995, p. 226.

17. Quoted in Niall Kilkenny, "Giants in the New World!!," Reformation Online, 2008. www.reformation.org.

Chapter Three: Giants in Popular Culture and the Arts

18. Joe Nickell, *Secrets of the Sideshows*. Lexington, KY: University Press of Kentucky, 2005, p. 81.

19. Arlen Pringle, e-mail message to author, May 23, 2011.

20. Richard Corliss, "Ponyo: More Ani-magic from Miyazaki," *Time*, September 2, 2008. www.time.com.

21. Pringle, e-mail.

22. L. Frank Baum, *The Tin Woodman of Oz*, Classic Authors, 2011. www.classicauthors.net.

23. Petronella Wyatt, "What Happened When Britain's Naked Giant Got a BIG Makeover," *Mail Online* (UK), September 16, 2008. www.dailymail.co.uk.

Chapter Four: Modern Times: Giants Both Alleged and Real

24. Greg Bishop et al., *Weird California*. New York: Sterling, 2006, p. 30.

25. Quoted in Radio Fiji Two, "Fiji Museum Finds Footprint Artifact," August 30, 2010. www.radiofiji.com.fj.

26. Alex Boese, "The Cardiff Giant," Museum of Hoaxes. www.museumofhoaxes.com.

27. Quoted in *ScienceDaily*, "Genetic Mutation Responsible for 'Gigantism' Disease—or Acromegaly—Identified," January 10, 2011. www.sciencedaily.com.

28. Quoted in Nikhil Swaminathan, "What Causes Gigantism?," *Scientific American*, August 14, 2008. www.scientificamerican .com.

29. Gina Kolata, "In a Giant's Story, a New Chapter Writ by His DNA," *New York Times*, January 5, 2011. www.nytimes.com.

30. Quoted in DeLoach, *Giants*, p. 11.

For Further Exploration

Books

Jeff Bahr and Janet Friedman, *Amazing and Unusual USA*. Lincolnwood, IL: Publications International, 2009.

Ann Bingham and Jeremy Roberts, *South and Meso-American Mythology A to Z*. New York: Chelsea House, 2010.

Corona Brezina, *Celtic Mythology*. New York: Rosen, 2008.

Kathleen Daly, *Norse Mythology A to Z*. New York: Chelsea House, 2010.

Zachary Hamby, *Greek Mythology for Teens: Classic Myths in Today's World*. Waco, TX: Prufrock, 2011.

Patricia Ann Lynch and Jeremy Roberts, *African Mythology A to Z*. New York: Chelsea House, 2010.

———, *Native American Mythology A to Z*. New York: Chelsea House, 2010.

Neil Philip, *Mythology*. New York: Dorling Kindersley, 2011.

Rob Waring, *The Giant's Causeway*. Washington, DC: National Geographic, 2008.

Websites

Encyclopedia Mythica (www.pantheon.org). This site divides descriptions of mythical beasts in several ways, including geographically and by type.

"Gallery of Huge Beings," World's Largest Roadside Attractions (www.wlra.us/hugebeings.htm). This entertaining site details some of the many giant statues that dot America's landscape.

"Giants," Theoi Greek Mythology (www.theoi.com/greek-mythology/giants.html). This site provides details on the Titans and the many other giants in Greek mythology.

"Mythical Creatures List," MythBeasts (www.mythbeasts.com/index.php). This site has short descriptions of many legendary creatures, including giants.

"Paul Bunyan," American Folklore (http://americanfolklore.net/folklore/paul-bunyan). A collection of colorful stories about America's most famous giant.

Index

Picture Credits

About the Author

Adam Woog has written many books for children, young adults, and adults. He lives in Seattle, Washington, with his wife, Karen Kent. Their daughter Leah is in university.